# spectacles

shome dasgupta

word west press | brooklyn, new york

isbn: 978-1-7369477-3-9

published by word west in brooklyn, ny

first us edition 2021

printed in the usa

www.wordwest.co

cover photo:

cover & interior design: word west

When you're around I stuff my mouth with cloth and hope to drown. Sometimes I hope you drown. Sometimes I hope we drown together, that I drown. Sometimes I hope you drown. Sometimes I hope we drown together.

There was a time when we were spectacular. We are now quiet and unending. I can't hear you anymore—I can see right through you: you are air and you are nothing, and there is nothing between us.

You know I was never good with attention and you were never good with giving me what I want. You knew what I wanted, or what, you knew what I didn't want.

Bygones. And you never, never said bye. You keep going like I am everything to you. Why? What makes me so special? What makes me so good?

What do you think about that? Do you like it? Or is it killing you?

I don't want you. And what makes this more fun is that you want me.

I'm not sure if I'll ever tell you the time I tried to kill you. Who knows—maybe later on I'll tell you, most probably when you'll do something sweet for me.

Maybe I was hoping that you'd catch me trying to kill you and then you'd kill me instead. I would have loved that. You'd come off as such a fucking jerk.

When you were away, I'd spit on
them or tear some of the leaves
or pour orange juice into them
or break off some of the stems in
hopes they wouldn't make it.

You looked so vulnerable when
you were watering the plants.

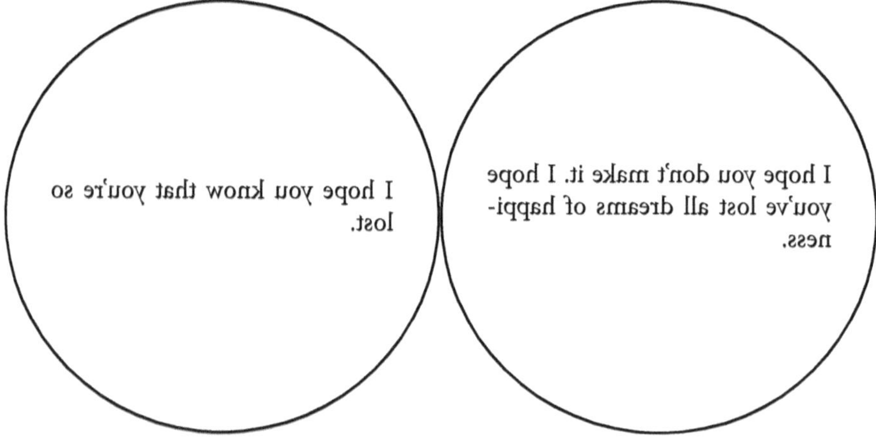
I hope you know that you're so lost.
I hope you don't make it. I hope you've lost all dreams of happiness.

I've met better, had better, done better. You're really nothing special. You're actually boring.

I hope you realize that you're no good. I never said that I was any good, and I guess you never said you were either, but just know that you aren't anything special.

This is nothing at all and I can't wait until you realize this and realize that we were just a waste of our time—that you are just a waste of my time.

Grow up. Love is such a childish thing and you are such a child. This isn't a fairy tale.

When I look away you still look
at me I can tell and it's annoying.
And you're annoying.

We used to look at each other.
like we were strangers. We look
at each other like we are each
other.

I asked you about things, and you would never answer. I understood what you said.

What do you think about when you think about me? When I think about you, I think about me.

I remember that. "Lily pads," you would say and walk back inside to check on me. I saw you through the window. We were such great gaggers, you and I.

Remember the pond and how the lily pads drifted into each other when the wind came. We ate pancakes soon after, and we threw up for two days. You would always let me go first, and sometimes you couldn't wait, and went in the backyard while the neighbors stared at you.

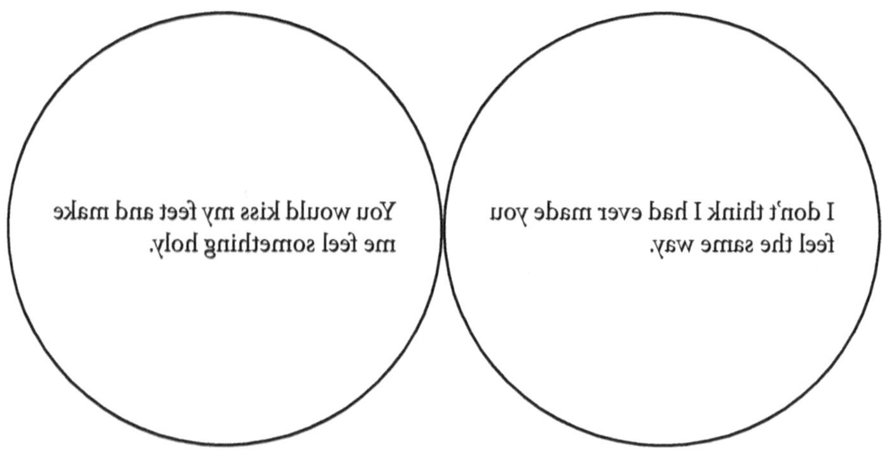
You would kiss my feet and make me feel something holy.
I don't think I had ever made you feel the same way.

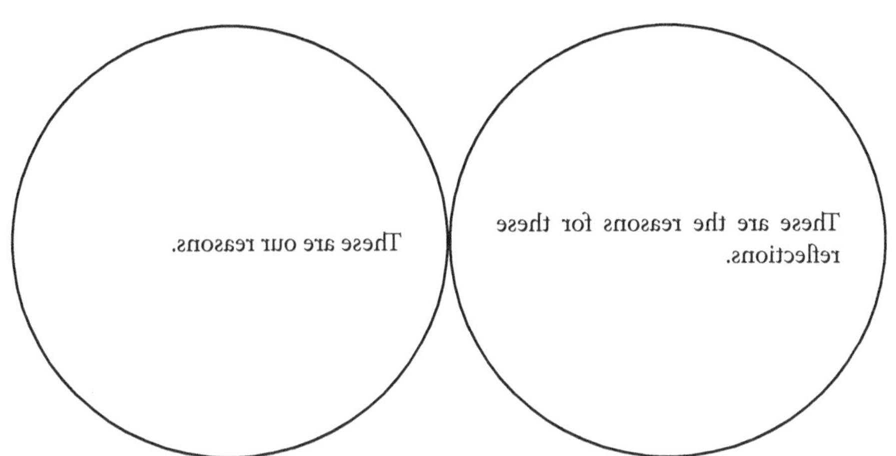
These are our reasons.
These are the reasons for these reflections.

Can you see me? Feel me. Let me go. Go away. Don't look at me. Look at me. Why?
Why? Why don't you hate me the way I hate myself?

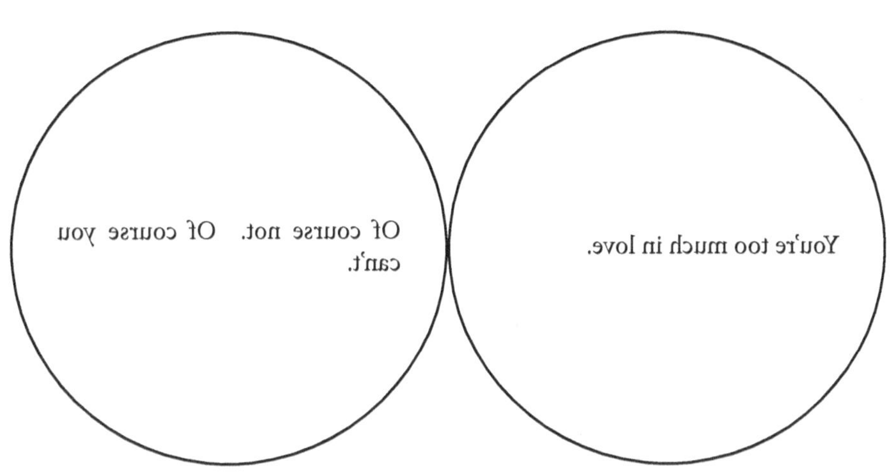
Of course not.   Of course you can't.
You're too much in love.

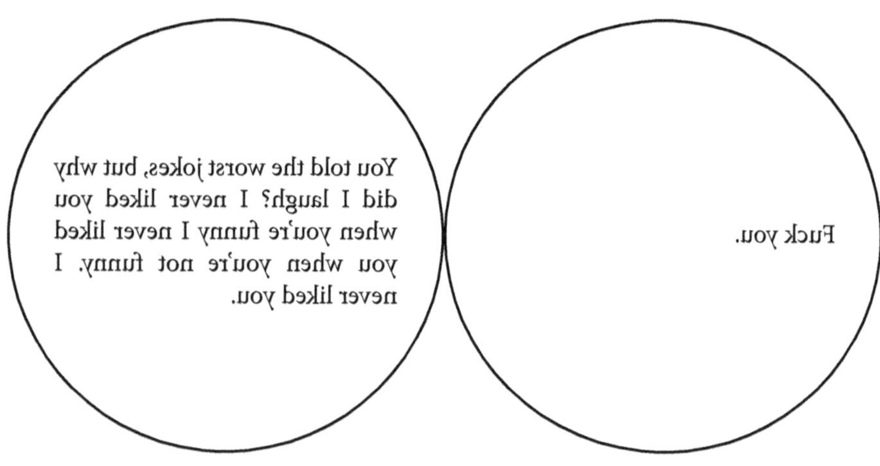

You told the worst jokes, but why
did I laugh? I never liked you
when you're funny I never liked
you when you're not funny, I
never liked you.

Fuck you.

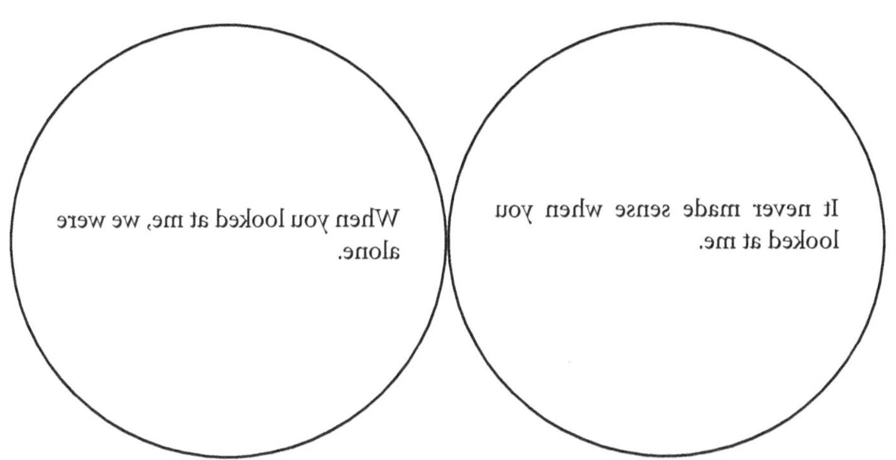
When you looked at me, we were alone.
It never made sense when you looked at me.

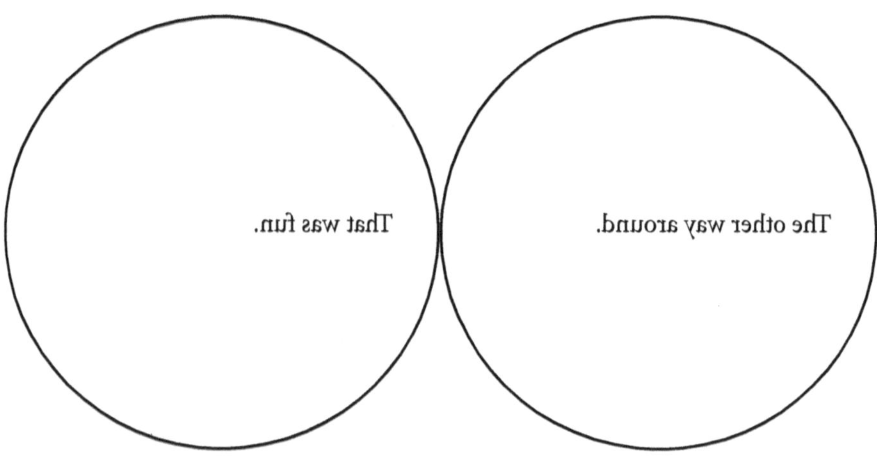
That was fun.
The other way around.

Why did you like the things I did when I did those things to make you hate me? Our arguments weren't even arguments. It was me screaming and you looking at me like you do when we're in bed.

Sometimes I would just throw everything at you—clothes, spoons, plates, chairs, and all you would do is pick them up and put them back in place and tell me you love me. Can you see me? There is this block of air—can you see it? I'm right here in front of you, can you see me? I've never stood like this before. I've never let you know before.

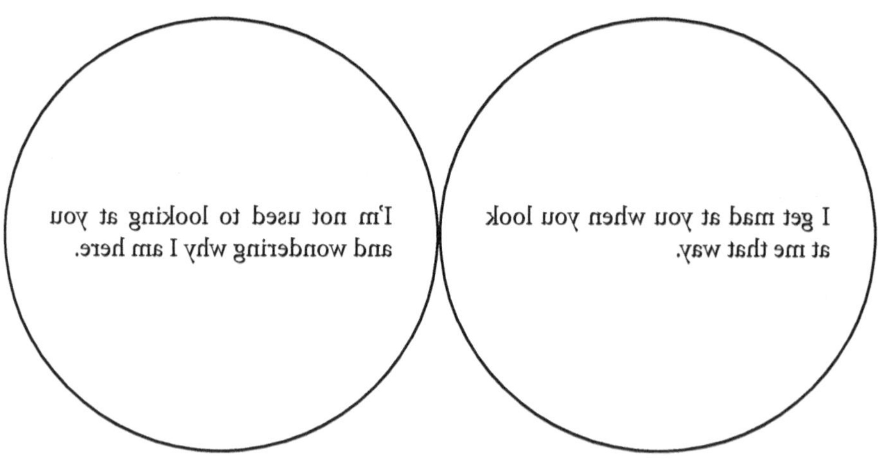

I'm not used to looking at you
and wondering why I am here.
I get mad at you when you look
at me that way.

Sometimes I see myself cutting a circle around me, and I fall through, going towards the middle of the earth, but then you grab me and pull me back up. Why would you want to pull me back up?

Leave me alone.

You make me feel like a ghost
when I want to be invisible.
When I'm invisible, I want to be
held. No one has ever held me
like you, and I didn't like it when
you would let go.

And it's because of things like
that that I wanted to look away.

You don't know this, but I saw you cry once. It was the one and only time I've seen you do this. You were in the bedroom, and I guess you didn't hear me coming in through the front door.

You were sitting on the bed with your back to me, and I could hear these whimpers and sniffles, and I wanted to be there for you, but I realized that you were most probably crying because of something I did. Usually I laugh when people cry but that time, all I could do was stare at the back of your neck.

When the sun has not set itself to sit, in this medium, I open my eyes and see nothing but fields of sensations symbolized by your fingertips, and I wish for a shooting star to put a bullet in my chest so I can live longer and without thought. Once, I was at a wishing well, and I wished you well, but in this hydrated chimney, I threw a penny and it refused to go down.

It floated, not wanting to drown, not wanting to be surrounded by dreams and copper that sleep on the ocean floor, waiting to be fed by more oxidized gleam. It didn't make me smile, but I did wonder, I did hope, that pennies would be real, and I was just a nightmare.

We were so glorious when we walked outside, under the sun. Everything was in such splendor during those times—hand in hand, not saying anything, but just walking and walking until we started stumbling down because of earth's curvature. Golden. Golden warmth—a blanket that was protecting you from me, I think, and when the light went away, you protected me from darkness.

Remember when that funny looking guy asked us if "we do," and we both said, "I do," and then the next day "we didn't."

The earth was frozen that one day—when we woke up around 11 and decided to get some coffee from the Laundromat. It was April, and we walked four blocks in our robes. We were royalty without thrones. We were rich peasants.

I've always wanted to eat your earlobes and lick your elbows and feel the grit of your tongue against all the hate that I have for you.

Not too long ago, I read all the letters you had written to me throughout the past 12 years. I remember falling in love with paper with each word traveling from those crumply sheets to my head.

As I read them again, all I could think about is how you're such a little child with no clue. And look at you now, reading this, I wish I was here, just to see the re-flections of this. How poor you'd look, I imagine.

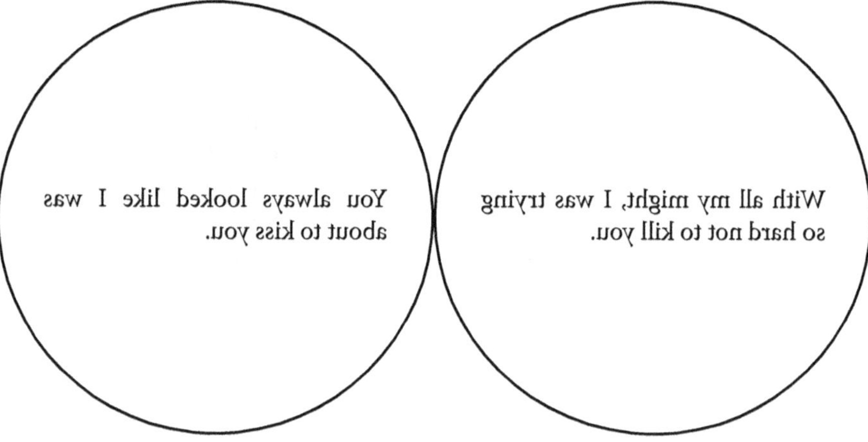
You always looked like I was
about to kiss you.

With all my might, I was trying
so hard not to kill you.

When we were in bed, trying to fall asleep, I would look at you sometimes and study your face—its creases and protrusions, the curvatures and indentions—and whenever you inhaled through your nose, I would do the same, like I was trying to be one with you. How could you sleep so peacefully? When you would exhale, I would cough.

You never woke up though, and I would get out of bed and smoke cigarettes outside. When I would come back in, I would find you sprawled over my side of the bed. I thought that you never noticed I was gone. But I finally realized what you meant, when you randomly said, "I roll over and have nightmares," while we were eating donuts.

I wish you cheated on me. I wish you never listened to me. I wish you were everything I didn't want. I wish we never met. I wish we could stay naked forever.

You are everything I never wanted.

Go away, I don't ever want to see you anymore. Are you crying? Cry.

Cry like you care. It means nothing to me. Your tears. Your feelings. Your thoughts and dreams.

I would have this repeating dream that we were tigers and when we looked at each other our black stripes would fly away from our skin and transform into ashes and come back down on our heads.

I dreamt you were real. And I was just in your imagination, that I didn't really exist. I wish I didn't. I wish you weren't. I wish we were all dead and happy.

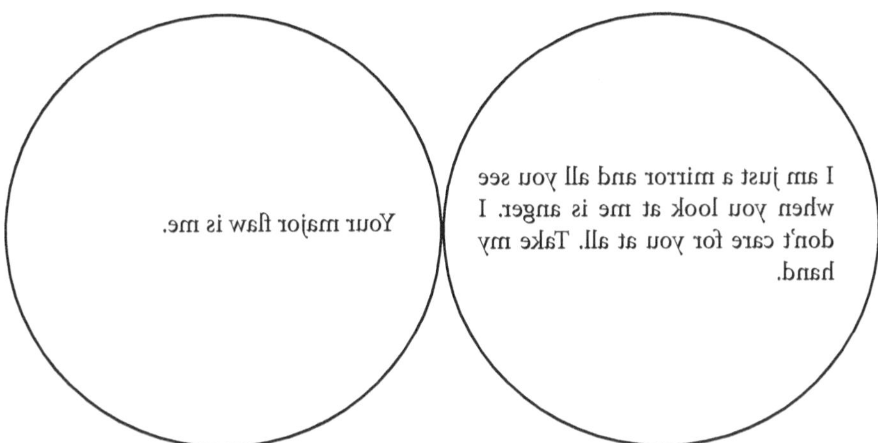
Your major flaw is me.

I am just a mirror and all you see when you look at me is anger. I don't care for you at all. Take my hand.

You have so many flaws. You're such an idiot. There is so much wrong with you.

Your love for silence always made me want to shout through a megaphone into your ear di-rectly. But you always heard me anyway.

Sunlight. Sunlight. Sunlight. Sunlight.
Sunlight. Sunlight. Sunlight. Sunlight.
Sunlight. Sunlight. Sunlight. Sunlight.
Sunlight. Sunlight. Sunlight. Sunlight.
Sunlight. Sunlight. Sunlight. Sunlight.
Sunlight. Sunlight. Sunlight. Sunlight.
Sunlight. Sunlight. Sunlight. Sunlight.
Sunlight. Sunlight. Sunlight. Sunlight.
Sunlight. Sunlight. Sunlight. Sunlight.
Sunlight. Sunlight. Sunlight.

Morning. Morning. Morning. Morning.
Morning. Morning. Morning. Morning.
Morning. Morning. Morning. Morning.
Morning. Morning. Morning. Morning.
Morning. Morning. Morning. Morning.
Morning. Morning. Morning. Morning.
Morning. Morning. Morning. Morning.
Morning. Morning. Morning. Morning.
Morning. Morning. Morning.

If only we were just turtles, if
only we had shells on our backs
that could take us away from this
world.

If only we could exist in darkness
so that we never have to look at
each other. Never look at me,
never again.

I hated waking up because I knew you would be there. I tried reading your thoughts. I wish I could have hidden everything from you, but you always found it all, even if you weren't looking for anything.

I feel bad for you.

When we showered together, lathering each other, I wondered if you ever had the guts to shove a bar of soap down my throat so that I would choke on such a sweet scent.

I wish you would have. I would have never done that to you, but you should have done that to me.

We lived inside the stomachs of ghosts, wandering from one side to the other side, hoping that we would be released through their mouths so that we could fly away into a realm where we would have never known each other.

Most of the time I thought you were just a sick walrus on the beach waiting to die. You would try to flap your flippers. You would look at me, as if you'd think I would help you, as if you'd think that I cared for you.

44

We would wake up dead with our
bones strewn about the kitchen.
The tea kettle bellowing on the
stove. Our skulls clattering in
unison.

We no longer had to live as
we gazed into the sink. The
drips from the faucet em-
phasized the beginnings of
our silent lives.

Sometimes I could feel mildew
growing against the inner walls
of my skull—all that could grow
from my decaying thoughts.

Drip. Drip. Drip. Drip. Drip.
Drip. Drip. Drip. Drip. Drip.
Drip. Drip. Drip. Drip. Drip.
Drip. Drip. Drip. Drip. Drip.
Drip. Drip. Drip. Drip. Drip.
Drip. Drip. Drip. Drip.

"I love you."
"You are my sunshine."
"You're so pretty."
"I want to hold you forever."
"I want to kiss you right now."

Who the fuck says those kinds of things anymore? You would. Because you're just a clueless little walrus. Because you're just an idiot looking for help. Because you believe in love.

I love how you always look both
ways before crossing the street,
and sometimes you would look
at me like I should want to hold
your hand.

I want to walk into your eyes and live inside of you to see what you're all about.
Organ by organ, I want to dissect you
and realize that maybe you're not human.
Are you? I don't think I've ever asked you
before. Are you human? I want to travel
from one blood cell to another until I've
covered all of your innards. You would
probably feel some kind of darkness
growing inside of you.

That one night when I punched a hole in the wall, you didn't even say anything. It was like your silence was harsher than some-thing you should have said.

The fire from your lips bringing flames of despair—I turn my head as your words singe my hair. We are pain in gentle sips. Our brains are full of fervor.

To dawn's dust, we stride to morning sun, hoping for a new world. But every time I look at you, I know all you see is history. We are birds, and when we flap our wings, all we do is fall. This is it. *No more wings.*

We are glimpses.

You can never make me happy.
You can never do anything right.
You can never let go of me.

—Don't send me any more letters,
washed up love letters, poems,
or whatever else it is that goes
through your mind—thinking it
will make me happy.

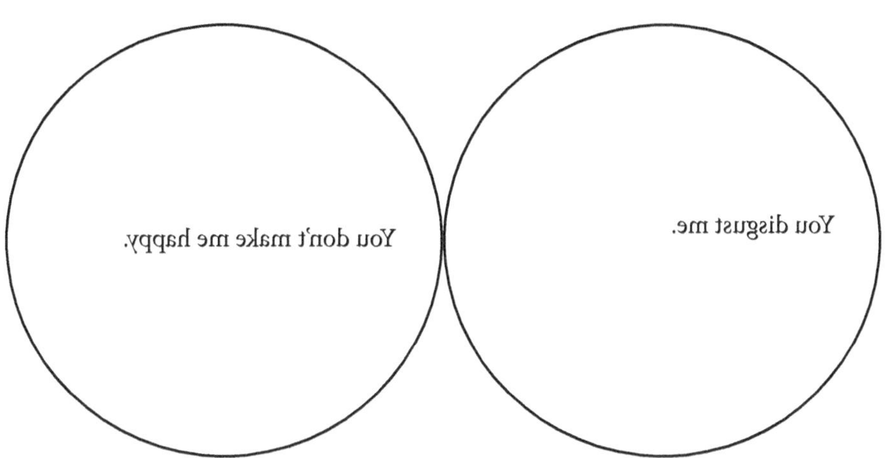

You don't make me happy.
You disgust me.

I'm imagining the reflection of what you're seeing here right now.

I'm imagining the pain and hurt you're feeling right now—and I'm loving it.

We were the vibrant sounds of dreams in slumber. But now we are just shrouds. We are caked pots and pans, rusted and dim and dull.

We were something magnificent. We had the world in our mouths.

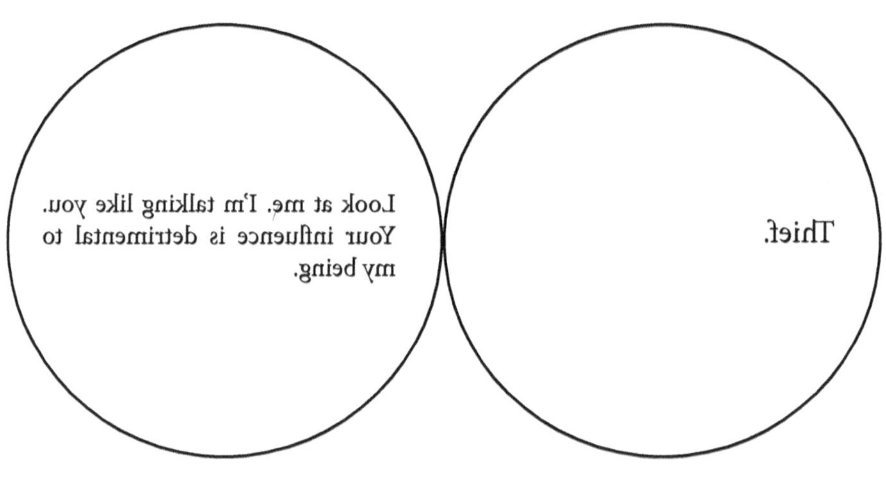
Look at me. I'm talking like you.
Your influence is detrimental to
my being.
Thief.

We are mute. We breathe
iron-oxide. We chip away.

Sometimes I look at my own eyes
and wait for them to disappear.
Sometimes I collapse into air.

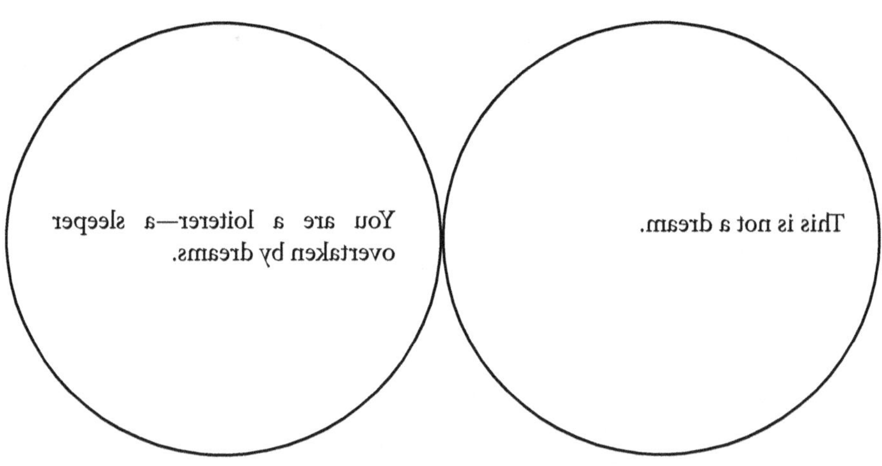
You are a loiterer—a sleeper overtaken by dreams.
This is not a dream.

And when our mouths are open
and all we hear is that rushing
air, we are two blind people not
wanting to close our mouths.

We have yawned a million-year
yawn.

Remember those ventriloquists we saw at the theater a few years ago? I wished that I could do that to you. I wish I could make you talk and say things that I wanted to hear.

I wanted to be so unhappy. I wish I could make you shut-up.

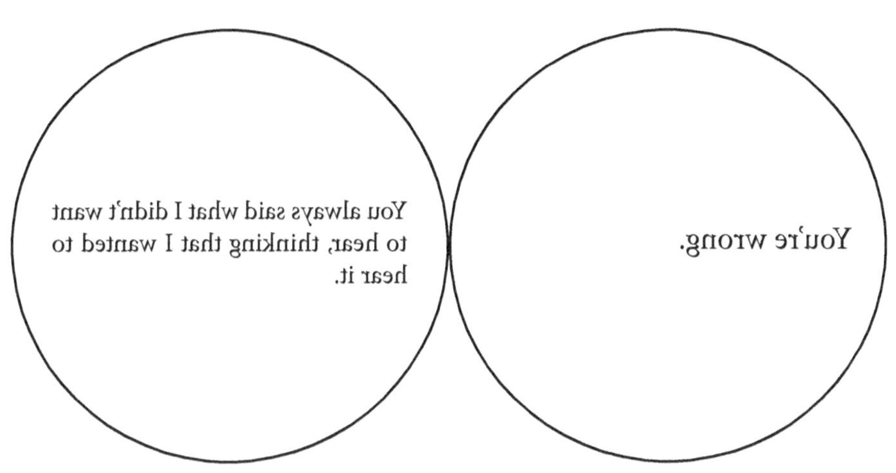
You always said what I didn't want
to hear, thinking that I wanted to
hear it.

You're wrong.

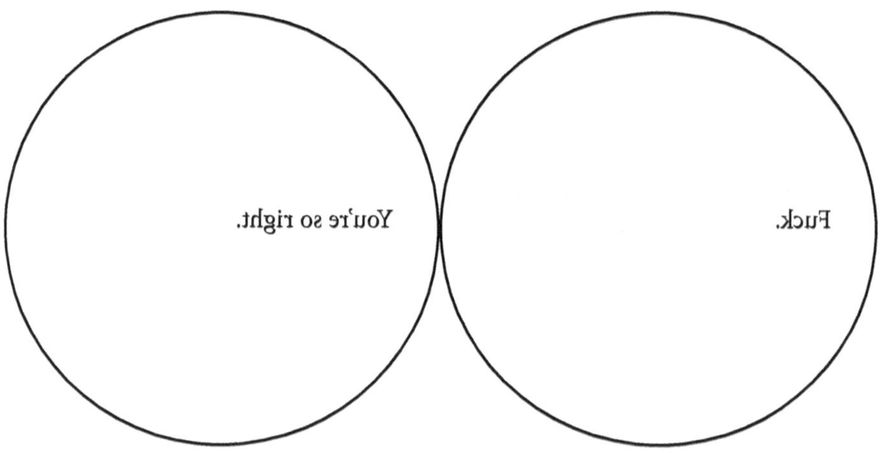
You're so right.
Fuck.

I don't have any friends. Any family. There was no one else to make sure I was okay, other than you. I never thanked you for doing that.

When I was really sick and could barely stand up or talk or even breathe for that matter, you took care of me. Don't think I don't remember that. I do. I have no one.

Exactly four years ago, you fell from the balcony and broke your wrists. How did it happen? You were trying to keep me from jumping off. I'm glad I didn't. After seeing you walking around with so much pain in those casts, I realized it wouldn't have been worth it, though I was actually thinking I wouldn't come out alive after the jump.

You saved my life, didn't you?

How many times have you saved my life?

What kind of hero are you to save a life that should be taken away by some kind of villain.

You would have just shrugged your shoulders and looked at me like you were ready to go to sleep. Though you have so many things, you were always willing to part with them, like when you sold your bicycle so you could buy me those jeans. They were way too expensive. I'm wearing them right now.

I've thought about throwing all of your things away or burning them or selling them. Your movies, books, music, and clothes, and your photo albums, memorable keepsakes, especially things that I never gave you—I've thought about getting rid of all them. Only because I just wanted to see how you would react. I wanted to see you at your worst, though it probably wouldn't have caused any kind of extreme emotion out of you.

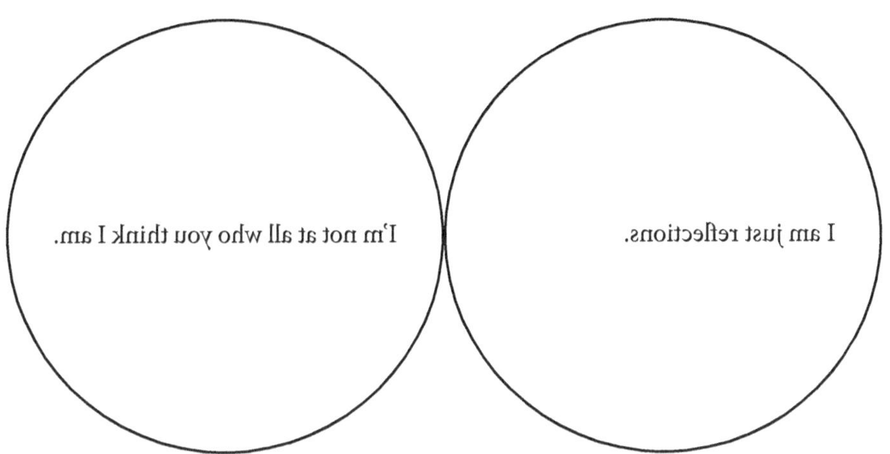

I'm not at all who you think I am.
I am just reflections.

When you were with me, I felt nothing, but in a good way.

I'm such a pompous trumpet, and you wear your eyes like a street mutt. And you sound so sad when you turn your head this way and that, just looking to be loved. Pathetic. Just pathetic. You are so pathetic.

I look up from time to time, but never see what I want to see. Have you seen him? He was crazy and fucked up and lost. But for some reason you thought he was going somewhere. You two had the same eyes.

Remember the man with feathers stuck in his hair who walked around our block, asking for a beak. He came around every Sunday. And you made a beak out of papier mâché and gave it to him. We never saw him since. I wonder if he's actually flying.

Fridays must have been the worse for you—I would come home late from work, and you would stay up until I came back even though you had to get up in three hours to go to your Satur-day shift. You're so dumb.

You could've just slept. Everyone else would have. You aren't like anyone else, and that's where you messed up. I didn't talk to you when I got home.

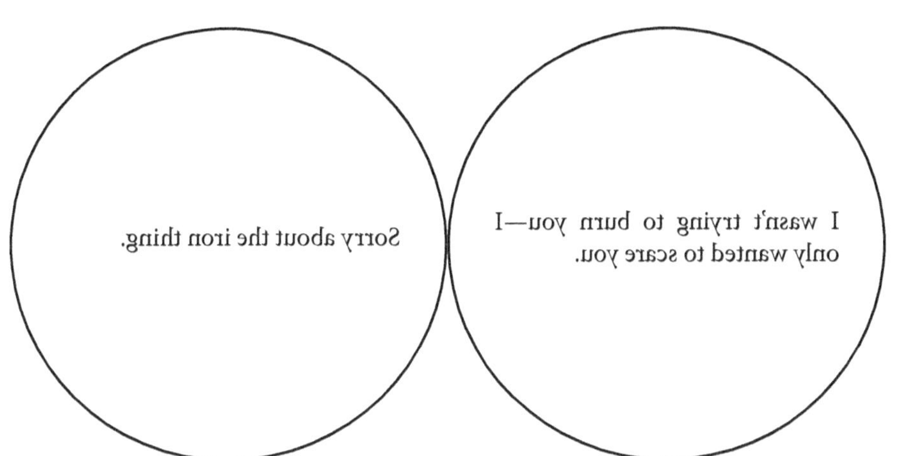
Sorry about the iron thing.
I wasn't trying to burn you—I
only wanted to scare you.

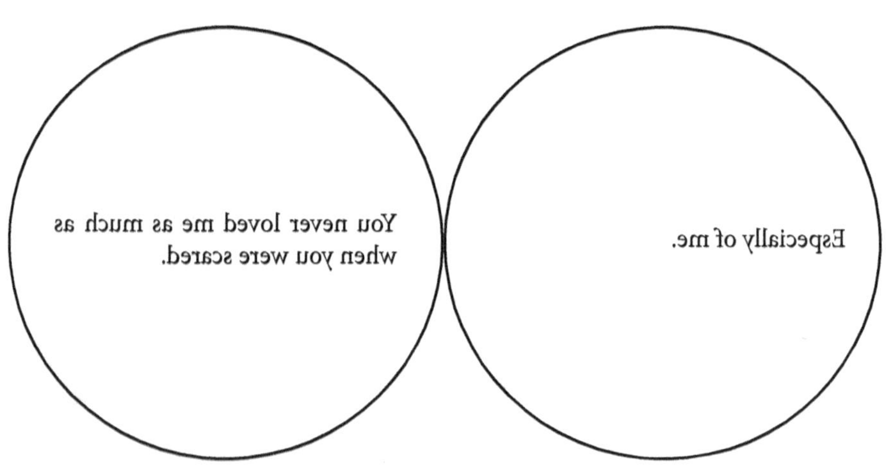
You never loved me as much as when you were scared.

Especially of me.

This must be the first thing you've read written by me, for you. Not what you expected, I'm sure. I'm sure you are thinking wonderful things about me even though I want nothing to do with you, even though you are the worst thing to have ever happened in my life.

I had written letters to you—love letters or poems or whatever, but I never gave them to you. I have them all stored in a box. They would probably make you so happy, but I don't want to give you that chance of being pleased.

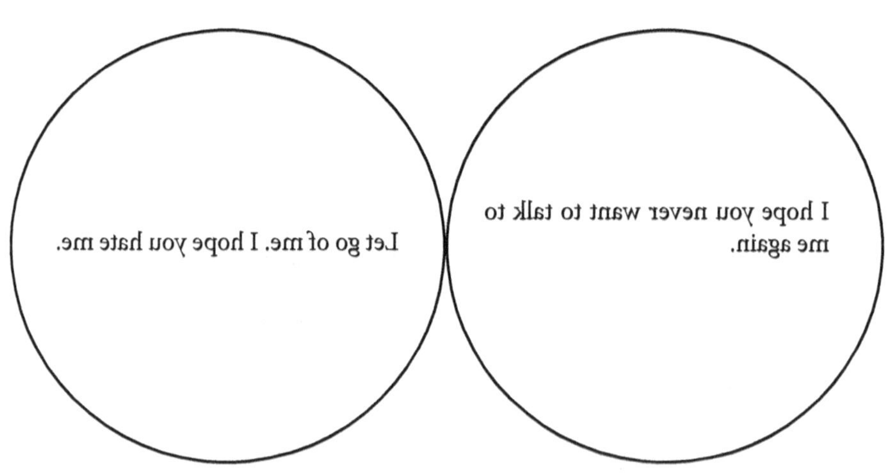
Let go of me. I hope you hate me.
I hope you never want to talk to me again.

Don't think I'm lying, these are all truths.
You know I can't lie unless it's to your face.

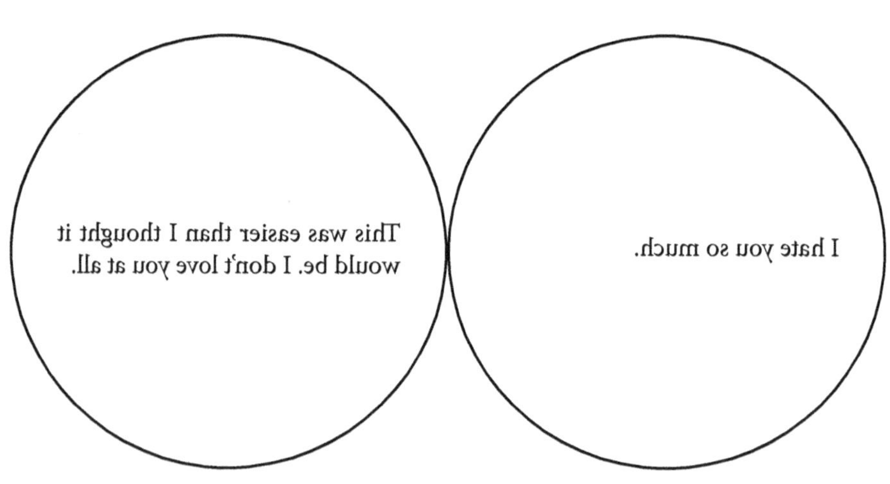
This was easier than I thought it would be. I don't love you at all.
I hate you so much.

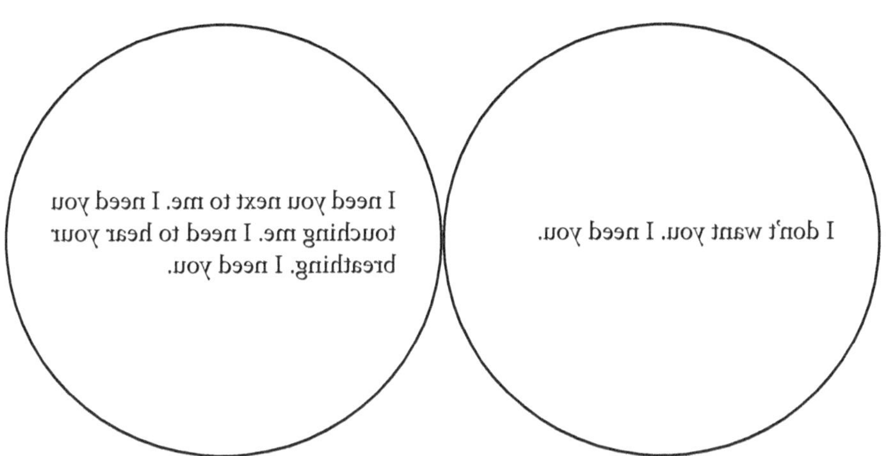
I need you next to me. I need you touching me. I need to hear your breathing. I need you.
I don't want you. I need you.

In the evenings, when we would
sit in the living room and stare at
the wall, and pretend that everything outside wasn't there.

I always thought about giving
you a hug.

Our tongues were antennae. Our eyes closed. Our minds closed. The touching. The feeling. The skin against skin.

Our tongues were antennae. Our tongues.

You have a horrible voice. When I couldn't sleep and you sang lullabies to help me close my eyes, I wanted to laugh right in your face because of your terrible voice.

I wanted to tell you to never sing again. I could never do it though because I would always fall asleep.

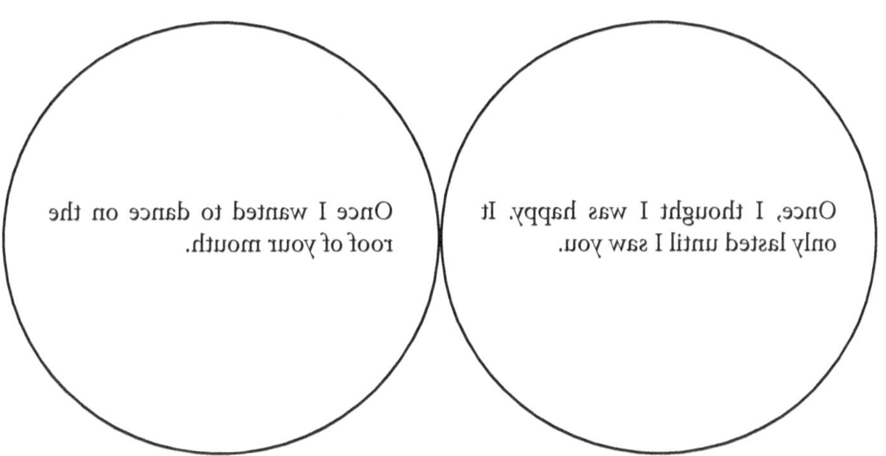
Once I wanted to dance on the
roof of your mouth.

Once, I thought I was happy. It
only lasted until I saw you.

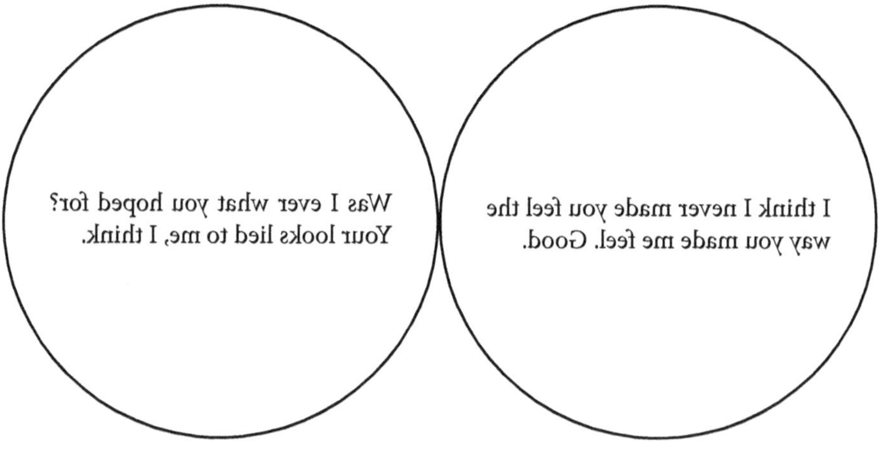

Was I ever what you hoped for?
Your looks lied to me, I think.

I think I never made you feel the
way you made me feel. Good.

But you never lied to me, I know.
I know how I make you feel, and
I refuse to think about it. Why?

Because I don't want to realize
that I exist. I don't want to understand the idea that you exist.

Tell me I'm wrong. Tell me I'm right. Tell me something I don't want to hear.

Tell me there was a time when we would know everything to know about each other and still look at each other like we were discoveries.

We were certainly something.

We knew how to live a life where one and one blended into some kind of chaotic clump of energy, full of spectrums of every gamut that ever existed. Nothing could live up to us. No one could imagine what we were. Are. Are. Are. Are. Are. Are.

What are you seeing now? I can only see blurs—watery and stringy and woozy, like I'm on a ship, rocking, wanting to gag all over the world until everything and everyone has eroded and it's just us. We are the greatest gag of all.

What am I trying to say? I never know what I'm trying to say but you always know what I mean. So, tell me. Tell me what this means. Help me out. I fucking hate you. No one has ever loved me the way you did and I will never forgive you for that. Understand.

I wish I'm actually here right in front of you. I can rip this up as you read it. I want to rip your memories. I want to rip your skin. I want to show you what I have in the palm of my hand. I want to tell you secrets. I want to rip your arms off and put them in my pocket. I want nothing but you.

I miss your glasses.

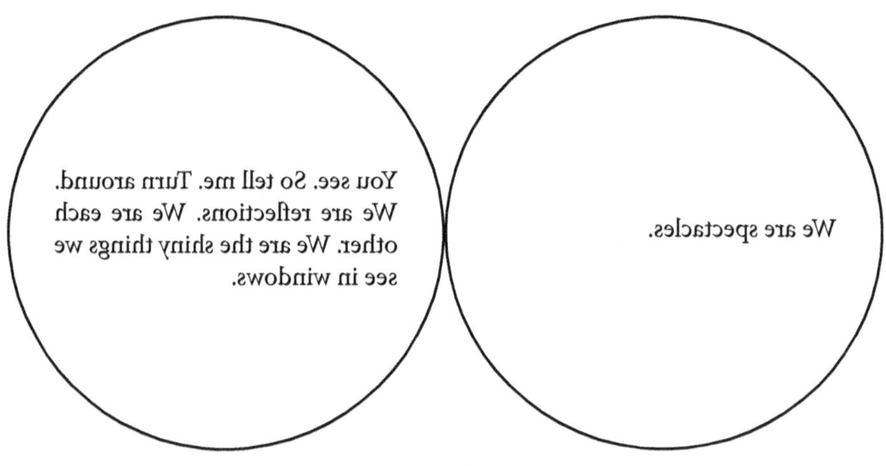
You see. So tell me. Turn around.
We are reflections. We are each
other. We are the shiny things we
see in windows.

We are spectacles.

Shome Dasgupta is the author of *i am here And You Are Gone* (Winner Of The 2010 OW Press Contest), *The Seagull And The Urn* (HarperCollins India), *Anklet And Other Stories* (Golden Antelope Press), *Pretend I Am Someone You Like* (Livingston Press), *Mute* (Tolsun Books), *Spectacles* (Word West), and a poetry collection, *Iron Oxide* (Assure Press, 2021). His fiction, poetry, and creative nonfiction have appeared in *McSweeney's Internet Tendency*, *Hobart*, *New Orleans Review*, *Redivider*, *New Delta Review*, *Necessary Fiction*, *New World Writing*, *Parentheses Journal*, *Magma Poetry*, and elsewhere. His fiction and poetry have been anthologized in *Best Small Fictions 2019* and *Best Small Fictions 2021* (Sonder Press), *The &Now Awards 2: The Best Innovative Writing* (&Now Books), and *Poetic Voices Without Borders 2* (Gival Press). His work has been featured as a *storySouth* Million Writers Award Notable Story, and his stories and poems have been nominated for the Pushcart Prize, Best Small Fictions, Best Of The Net, and the Orison Anthology. He is currently the series editor of the *Wigleaf* Top 50. He took part in the Innovative Fiction panel, as a featured author, at the Louisiana Book Festival. He lives in Lafayette, LA and can be found at www.shomedome.com and @laughingyeti.